THE LITTLE FISH THAT GOT AWAY

Story by **BERNADINE COOK**

Pictures by Crockett Johnson

SCHOLASTIC INC.
New York Toronto London Auckland Sydney

ISBN 0-590-01503-6

39 38 37 36 35 34 33 32 31 30   6 7 8 9/8 0/9

Printed in the U.S.A.   07

Once upon a time

there was a boy

who liked to go fishing.

There he goes,

over there on the other page.

He went fishing every day.

But he never,

no never,

got any fish.

All he ever did catch

was a bad cold.

But ONE day . . .

. . . he dug some worms,

and he put them in a can,

and he got his fish pole.

Then off he went with his fish pole.

He came to the place he liked best.

He put a worm on the pin,

and he put the pin in the water,

and he waited

—and waited

and waited.

Then he saw

a GREAT GREAT big fish.

It swam around, and around,

and around, and around,

and around and around

and around.

Like this.

It looked at the worm on the pin.

It wiggled its

GREAT GREAT big tail.

Then it swam

around, and around,

and around and around

and around

—right back where

it came from.

Just like this.

The boy

waited

and waited

—and waited.

Then along came

a GREAT big fish.

And it swam around,

and around, and

around and around

and around.

Just like this.

It looked at the worm on the pin.

It wiggled its GREAT big tail.

Then it swam

around, and around,

and around and around

and around

—right back where

it came from.

Just like this.

The boy

waited

and waited

—and waited.

Then along came

a BIG fish.

And it swam around,

and around, and

around and around

and around.

Like this.

It looked at the worm on the pin.

It wiggled its BIG tail.

Then it swam

around, and around,

and around and around

and around

—right back where

it came from.

Just like this.

So,

the boy

waited

and waited

—and waited.

Then along came

a LITTLE fish.

And it swam around,

and around, and

around and around

and around.

Just like this.

It looked at the worm on the pin.

It wiggled its LITTLE tail.

Then it swam

around, and around,

and around and around

and around

—right back where

it came from.

Just like this.

The boy was sad.

"I will not catch any fish

today," he said.

Then he looked down

—into the water.

And there in the water was
the GREAT GREAT big fish
coming back again.

It swam around, and around,
and around and around
and around.

It looked at the worm
on the pin.
It wiggled its GREAT GREAT big tail
Then —

—it ate the worm.

And the boy pulled

the GREAT GREAT big fish

out of the water

—and put him in the basket

under the tree.

He put another worm on the pin,

and he put the pin in the water,

and soon

the GREAT big fish

came back again.

It swam around and around.

It looked at the worm

on the pin.

It wiggled its GREAT big tail.

Then—

—it ate the worm.

And the boy pulled

the GREAT big fish

out of the water

—and put him in the basket

under the tree.

He put another worm on the pin,

and he put the pin in the water,

and soon

the BIG fish

came back again.

It swam around and around.

It looked at the worm

on the pin.

It wiggled its BIG tail.

Then—

—it ate the worm.

And the boy pulled

the BIG fish

out of the water

—and put him in the basket

under the tree.

He put another worm on the pin,

and he put the pin in the water,

and waited

and waited

—and waited.

And soon the LITTLE fish came
back again.

It swam around, and around,
and around and around
and around.

Like this.

It looked at the worm
on the pin.
It wiggled its little tail.
It looked at the worm again.

The boy sat very still.

"Hurry up, little fish,

and eat the worm.

Then I will go home

and show Mother and Father

all my fish."

But—

—would the little fish

bite the worm?

It looked and looked.

And then it looked again.

And then it swam around,

and around,

and around and around and around

—right back

where it

came from.

That made the boy

LAUGH

and laugh.

Then he picked up his basket with

the GREAT GREAT big fish in it

and the GREAT big fish in it

and the BIG fish in it.

And he went home.

Like this.

When he got home,

he showed his mother

the fish.

She was very happy

to have the fish.

She cleaned them,

and cooked them

for supper that night.

His father ate the GREAT big fish.

His mother ate the BIG fish.

And the boy ate

the GREAT GREAT big fish,

because he was so hungry.

Then the boy told

how he got the fish,

and how the little fish

would not eat the worm

on the pin.

And they all laughed and laughed

about the LITTLE fish

that

got

away.